Text copyright © 1996 Fox Busters Ltd
Illustrations copyright © 1996 Frank Rodgers

First published in Great Britain in 1996 by
Macdonald Young Books
an imprint of Wayland Publishers Ltd
61 Western Road
Hove
East Sussex
BN3 1JD

Reprinted in 1996 and 1998

Typeset in Bembo by Goodfellow & Egan, Cambridge
Printed and bound in Belgium by Proost International Book Co.

British Library Cataloguing in Publication Data available.

ISBN: 0 7500 2017 2

Dick King-Smith
MRS JOLLIPOP

Illustrated by Frank Rodgers

MACDONALD YOUNG BOOKS

"I wish I was still at school," said Mrs Jolly to her ginger cat.
"You're a bit old for that, aren't you?" said the cat.
"No, I don't mean I wish I was a child at school again," said
Mrs Jolly. "Goodness, that was fifty years ago. No, I mean I
wish I was still the school caretaker, like I used to be."

"But you retired, didn't you?" said the cat. "So that you could put your feet up and take things easy. Come to think of it, that's what you used to do at school."

Only the ginger cat knew that Mrs Jolly was actually a witch, with magic powers. When she had been the caretaker, and everyone else had gone home, she used to sit and drink tea while the vacuum cleaner and the polisher and the dustpan-and-brush did all the work for her.

"I know," said Mrs Jolly. "It's just the same here. I haven't got enough to do. But mostly I miss the children."

She opened her sweet tin (Mrs Jolly had a very sweet tooth) and took out a lollipop and began to suck it.

The ginger cat looked thoughtful, as cats do.

"How about being a lollipop lady?" he said.

"Outside the school, you mean? To see the children safely across the road?"

"Yes."

"But they've already got a lollipop lady."
"Not any more they haven't," said the ginger cat. "She's moving house. Her cat told me – he's a pal of mine."
So Mrs Jolly went to see the Headteacher, and the Headteacher rang up the Education Department. She told them what a marvellous caretaker Mrs Jolly had been and what a marvellous School Crossing Patrol (for that's what lollipop ladies are called) she would make. And Mrs Jolly got the job.

On her first morning she dressed up in her uniform – a long coat, the top half yellow, the bottom half white, and a black cap with a peak – and she picked up her long, striped pole on top of which was a big round white disc with an orange rim. This was her lollipop, and on it was written

The ginger cat stared silently at her, as cats do.
"Who are you staring at?" said Mrs Jolly.
"At Mrs Jolly the lollipop lady," said the cat. "I wonder what the children will call you now."

When the children came to school that morning, they were all
very pleased to see nice, friendly, cuddly Mrs Jolly again, with
her short nose and her two comfy round chins and her curly
brown hair going grey. On the pavement beside her sat her
ginger cat.

"Look!" they cried. "It's our Mrs Jolly! She's the new lollipop
lady! Hullo, Mrs Jolly!" and one of the smallest boys got
muddled and said "Hullo, Mrs Jollipop."

The ginger cat looked smug, as cats do.

At first Mrs Jolly behaved just like any other lollipop lady.
When a group of children had collected at the roadside, she
marched out into the middle of the road and held up her
lollipop. All the traffic stopped as Mrs Jolly shepherded the

children across. One of the biggest girls said to her "The traffic stops just as though that lollipop was a magic wand, doesn't it, Mrs Jollipop?" (for they all called her that now).

She did not know Mrs Jolly was really a witch.

"There's nothing magic about this lollipop," replied Mrs Jolly.
"But there could be," said the ginger cat, once the children had
all gone into school.
"How?" said Mrs Jolly.
"Put a spell on it," said the cat. "Turn it into a magic lollipop."
"Good idea," said Mrs Jolly.
She pointed a finger at the lollipop and did a funny little dance,
saying,

"Jumpety-jump,   hoppety-hop!
You're a magic lollipop."

"Come on," she said. "Let's go home," and she set off across the road, her lollipop held aloft, the cat at her heels. As they crossed, an approaching car stopped. The lady driving it stared in great surprise at Mrs Jolly's lollipop. Just for a second or two, it seemed to her it said

But when she looked again, it said

"I must get my eyes tested," she said to herself.

Next day Mrs Jolly began to have some more fun with her magic lollipop. The children never looked at it as they crossed the road, but several motorists got a shock.
Like a young man who was driving too fast and had to brake suddenly.

Just for a moment, it seemed the message on the lollipop was

Then there was a middle-aged man
who was puffing away at a large cigar.
He saw a different message for an
instant. It said

And lastly there was a very old man
driving an old and very dirty car,
that was covered in mud.
What he saw was

The young man looked slightly angry, the middle-aged man
looked more angry, and the old man very angry indeed.
Mrs Jolly looked amused.

"I shouldn't have suggested it," said the ginger cat when they got home.

"Making the lollipop a magic one, you mean?" said Mrs Jolly.

"Yes," said the cat. "It's going to get you into trouble, I can see it."

He looked disapproving, as cats do.

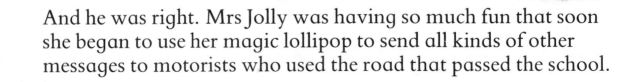

And he was right. Mrs Jolly was having so much fun that soon she began to use her magic lollipop to send all kinds of other messages to motorists who used the road that passed the school.

And of course the lollipop could send a message from either side of its disc. So an impatient-looking lady on one side, drumming her fingers on the steering-wheel, might see

While on the other side a lorry driver, yawning, could see

People with really wild messy hair were told to

GET A HAIRCUT

Very noisy people were told

QUIET PLEASE

Grumpy-looking people saw

CHEER UP

Sometimes the magic lollipop carried more general messages like

HAVE A NICE DAY

or

or

(just in case it was somebody's).

But the drivers who used that road and met the School Crossing Patrol would very often see – just for a second or two – a message on the disc of her lollipop that was definitely *not*

Twice each schoolday Mrs Jolly's ginger cat sat on the pavement and watched. He saw the worried looks on some drivers' faces as they peered at the lollipop. He saw them rub their eyes and peer again and shake their heads, before they drove on, looking bewildered. Sooner or later, he thought, someone will kick up a fuss about it, and then Mrs Jolly will get the sack. I must have a word with her about it.

And that evening he did.

"I suppose you're right," Mrs Jolly said. "It's a bit naughty of me. But I'll stop, I promise."

Mrs Jolly kept her word. After that her lollipop only ever said what it should. But the trouble with witches is they just can't resist using their magic powers.

One day, while Mrs Jolly was standing at the school crossing, waiting for the children, she remembered how she had put a spell on the school vacuum cleaner, and had ridden on it to win the Great Witches' Steeplechase. She looked at her lollipop. "I could have a ride on you if I wanted to," she said. "After all you're still my magic lollipop."

Just after she had seen the last lot of children across, there came a squealing of tyres, and then a car appeared, being driven very fast. It took no notice of Mrs Jolly and her lollipop but drove straight at her, so that she had to jump out of the way.

Some minutes later she heard a siren, and a police car came racing along and then braked to stop beside her.

"Have you seen a red car – two chaps in it – going very fast? They've just robbed a bank," said the driver.

"Yes," said Mrs Jolly. "Nearly ran me over. You'll have a job to catch them now."

But, she thought, as the police car sped away, I could soon
catch them, couldn't I?
She looked round. All the children had gone into school
and there was no one about.

Quickly Mrs Jolly put one leg on each side of the lollipop's pole
and grasped its disc like a steering-wheel.

"Lollipop, fly!
Up in the sky.
We'll clobber the robbers,
Will you and I,"

she chanted, and the ginger cat saw her blast off at
tremendous speed.

Zooming high above the streets (while far below people stared skyward, unable to believe their eyes), she quickly overtook the police car, and soon she saw the stolen car tearing along below.

Inside it, the two car thieves were laughing, confident that now the police would never catch them, when suddenly they got a horrible fright.

Flying along beside them – at seventy miles an hour – was a tubby lady dressed in a long coat, half yellow, half white, wearing a black cap on her curly brown hair going grey. She was shaking her head and wagging a finger at them.

They were so busy looking at Mrs Jolly and not at the road, that the car went straight through a hedge and finished up in someone's front garden.

Mrs Jolly hovered beside it like a helicopter until she saw the police car coming. Then she flew away, while the police arrested the dazed thieves.

"Oh Mrs Jolly!" sighed the ginger cat that evening, as they sat in the witch's cosy living room. "Whatever am I going to do with you? People are sure to have seen you flying about all over the town."

"Sorry," said Mrs Jolly. "I couldn't resist it. It was such fun. But I won't do it again."

She stood up, holding her lollipop and did a funny little dance, saying,

"Jumpety -jump,   hoppety -hop!

You're a normal lollipop."

"Don't worry," she said to the cat. "From now on I'm going to be as good as gold."

The ginger cat looked disbelieving, as cats do.

"Pigs might fly," he said.

"But not as well as witches,"
said Mrs Jolly, smiling.
It was a jolly smile.

Here are some more picture books by Macdonald
Young Books for you to enjoy:

The Jolly Witch
Written by Dick King-Smith · Illustrated by Frank Rodgers
Mrs Jolly is a school caretaker by day and a witch by night! She uses her magic
powers to help her clean the school – until one special night when she casts a
rather unusual spell on the vacuum cleaner.

Grimbledon Zoo is Closing Down
Written and Illustrated by Keith Brumpton
Grimbledon Zoo is closing down and there's to be an auction of all the animals.
Tina takes the hyena, Brian Ryan takes the lion – but some of the animals prove
to be a bit of a problem. Can the zoo be saved after all?

Baby Bear's Nose
Written by Penny McKinlay · Illustrated by Siobhan Dodds
Baby Bear isn't very pleased when he's told he's got his daddy's nose. So he sets
off in search of a nose that's just right for him.

There's a Monster Next Door!
Written and Illustrated by Peter Kavanagh
Robby Brown knows there's a monster next door, but nobody believes him.
So one day he decides to go and find out for himself . . .

For further information about these and other books, write to:
The Sales Department, Macdonald Young Books,
61 Western Road, Hove, East Sussex, BN3 1JD.